AMBAPALIKA

(A SHORT TALE)

RIYA KUSHWAHA

ISBN 979-888530685-0

to amrapali and kartik

Contents

Foreword   *vii*

Preface   *ix*

Acknowledgements   *xi*

Prologue   *xiii*

The Journey Wasn't Downhill

Note From The Author :-   11

FOREWORD

I wasn't amrapali until I met you......!

PREFACE

Hello myself, Amrapali I am courageous and powerful now. My life showed me different colors. After passing through each up and down, I could hardly survive. At last the only thought I would have was just to end myself, some days made me think that it's a cursed life which I got, but it is said that good things take time for me Mr. Kartik was the guardian angel. He gave me so much confidence due to which I am in this state now, from a broken hope to a new start he made me "Amrapali" who was somewhere lost in her life.

ACKNOWLEDGEMENTS

Thankyou Amrapali for being soo courageous and dealing with all the problems in a beautiful way. You are inspiration to all the girls out there. Who loose their confidence after being harassed or bonded. You had that boldness after being in so much pain you gave your 100% and was successful in escaping. Also you fought for you justice and took stand for yourself.

Also my special thanks to my parents, who raised me in a happy atmosphere, always supported my decisions, and also for setting my soul free towards my dreams.

Prologue

It is said that you get things which is defined in your fate may be, Mr. kartik was the only one for her.

The Journey Wasn't Downhill

I am Ambapalika, my father used to call me Amrapali. I was born in a small village in Andhra Pradesh and raised in a stereotypical atmosphere. I was not allowed to choose the path I wanted and I was always taught that " I am a girl and can never do anything without the support of a man". But a Hurricane of thoughts always surrounded my mind since the age of 10. It was not only me who was confronting these ordinances. Many others were also surviving the same kind of lifestyle. All of us had a fire in our eyes and wanted to somehow change the perception of people who accepted these sick laws from so many years ago. But we were unable to do so and were waiting for someone who could take a stand for us and set us free from these servitudes.

I was only 8 when my father passed away. He was the only one to whom I was close to. The day I got to know that my father is no more my heart broke into pieces it seemed to me that my heart and the blood of my emotion towards him were all ruptured. His dream was to see me growing willingly and without any bondage. He always taught me everything about how I could be dependent on myself and even admitted me in the school which was in the next village and was 25 km away from my village. He always took me on his black cycle with colorful beads. Sharing all ups and downs, sorrow and happiness and in the end, the day was always as cheerful as he was. I am not saying that my mother has never been a backbone to me but somewhere she lacked the support of society which she always wanted. Whenever she tried to raise me happily the taunts of the aunties and uncles of our village always pulled down the uprising thoughts of my mother. I accepted the truth that by staying here I can not be myself. "It is said that good things take time". These lines had great primacy in my life. People forced me to skip my studies and start taking care of household stuff as I was going to get married next year yes married....! I didn't even know the person, who was he or what was his work but yes it was decided by the people for whom I didn't have a bit of respect. I left my studies and started taking care of my family whenever I rejected to do so my mother had to face the consequences. I couldn't see that because of me my mother had to suffer a ton of reactions and everyone use to blame her and me for my father's death.

But No, everyone was wrong he was murdered because of the rental property issues. Yes, murdered he was unable to pay within the time limit. So those people would come to our house regularly, asking for money and then by giving serious threats would go back. We all thought they would co-operate with us but One day on Friday, Evening my father's phone rang. As he picked up the call someone warned him that either he pay it today or they'll come and take away the ladies present in the house. My father was afraid after listening to this he ran away asap to meet them and to ask for some few more days so that he could arrange the amount but they didn't listened and shot him and left behind my mother widow. Okay let us skip this topic otherwise I'll start sobering here.

Somehow the days flew I was 18 this year and my house was all decorated with " genda ke phools" yes it was my haldi all the guests and women present there were dancing as if, they are dancing in his/her child's marriage. I was completely out of my senses and was thinking how could I run away from this so far that no one can even find me. All the relatives were one by one coming towards me touching my face and saying " apne mard ko Pehali koshish me ladka hi dena " listening to this I stood up and directly moved inside my room everyone at my door were banging it and calling my name with a high pitch as if I have stolen something from there. My uncle was continuously yelling me out saying that "what will the relatives think about our family" I said I don't care. I pinched up his anger. He banged the door heavily and held my wrist tightly, dragging me right outside in the hall saying " sit quietly otherwise I'll give you a tight slap on your wretched face.

My mother was staring at me standing right beside me I can feel the pain she was going through. With tightened fists, she tried to suppress the tears in her eyes but was unable to do so and started whimpering in front of the whole crowd. My aunts took my mother into the kitchen with tight teeth she was saying to my mother to keep her mouth shut in front of everyone till the "Shaadi night and bidaai" gets over. Hahaha, the day when my dreams were going to be crushed was very close.

The evening of today was the day when I was getting married to a man I didn't even meet in my life. With all the makeup, jewelry, and yes that red lehenga I was taken to the venue the board which was hung there was decorated with white flowers, and " Amrapali weds Tanmay" was written with golden colors. I was shocked after reading this name the same name was in discussion as our friend circle was talking about a girl. She was raped by a 25-year-old man just after her marriage and was found dead on her bed the next morning and. I was aghast to see the same name I heard about I entered there everything was pretty good as if I was the most loved one in my family but no this was all the happiness they would be getting after sending me there. The groom was a man between 5.5-6.0 inches with a broad chest and heavy body. His aura could be easily defined and also the vibes he had made me feel insecure.

And the moment came when I was going to leave my house, in spite, it wasn't mine I was just living like a maid there. To be honest, not a single droplet of tears came into my eyes also I was thinking that was so disheartened that I am not feeling sad because of this act. But then too it didn't matter to me I am now stepping forward for a beautiful life and I was also curious to see my husband's reaction towards my pursuit

Everything was done now I reached my new home and was entering inside with a thought that here I might start a fresh journey with joy and freedom because this family seems to be a little supportive one, but before I know everyone nicely I can't conclude beforehand. I entered the room his sisters took me there. They used a white new bed sheet on the bed, beautified the room with white and red flowers, and suddenly a whisper came into my ears " will come and see this bedsheet tomorrow" they were his aunts who live in Mumbai. I called one of his sisters and asked why did all of them saying like this???. She elaborated to me all the sense behind this talk. She said this white bed sheet will define whether you are Virgin beforehand or not if the bloodstains are found on this bed sheet then you will pass your virginity test. I replied, what if I didn't bleed at that time, then? Then everyone will point out your character... She replied!

After hearing all this I was shocked I have never heard this kind of thing before...it made me think about my virginity I started thinking that what will happen to me if it doesn't ensue.

Everyone left me in the room and moved outside. I was alone sitting in my room waiting for him. I was so much nervous as I haven't seen the world and was not too big for all these things. Suddenly he entered the room put off his clothes and started wearing a new said to mc I am going to Lucknow for some work will be returning after 4 days... I asked ..we are married today itself only and you are going after listening to this " he slapped me on my face, saying you are here just to work and take care of me don't you ever dare to ask questions from me from now onwards" he slammed the door and moved away and left me crying. It seemed I have been thrown nearer to death by my family. Because the thought coming to my mind was only suicide, I was done with facing all the lows and problems in my life.

It's been 2 months of my married life but he didn't come back home from that day. Now I could barely spend one more day in this house. People here were acting as if they brought a maid or slave into this house, not a girl. I was always beaten for my cross questions. Whenever there would be a family meet up I was tied up with a rope in my room so that no one could know that I am here they didn't even let me eat properly. One day my father-in-law entered my room. I was terrified after seeing him I thought why did he come here he started opening the knot of rope and picked me up, for me it was a ray of hope I thought he is going to free me up but I was untrue he started forcing me to take off my clothes. I was afraid and started screaming so that anyone could listen and come inside my room, with an evil smile he replied, No one is in the house dear only you and me! I ran away to the main entrance so that I could escape but I was unable to do so he dragged me up through my legs, removed my clothes, continuously begging for my life and screaming as loud as I can so that anyone outside the house would listen. He poked my mouth and said sssshhhhhhh... Don't you dare to do anything and let me get cozy somehow the time passed, he was sleeping next to me I stood up and picked up my clothes and went in the bathroom turned on the shower, I was so much in pain that couldn't even able to walk and cried for 2 hours there. With staggering legs somehow I escaped myself outside the house while he was still in deep sleep, and nothing rather than this came into my mind. As I came out of the House one autorickshaw was standing as if he knew that I was coming without thinking anything, I said "bhaiya take me to the bus stop", he turned on the meter and took me there, I saw only one bus was parked there, without thinking anything, I entered inside and sat on the last seat then after a while a conductor came and stood next to me I was looking outside the window when he called madam Ji! I got scared and abruptly stood up saying," what you want from me, go from here!" He said, " are you mad or what I just need money for the ticket". I said bhaiya I don't have any money with me please take this earing and take it to the next stop please, he said please you better get off of this bus, They stopped the bus and pushed me out. With the aching abdomen, I was walking on the road I couldn't even see a single vehicle in that area and then I heard a sound of a motorcycle coming closer to me near and then nearer... As I turned back I saw that the motorcycle was at high speed I thought that it will collide with me but for god sake. The rider forcefully braked the motorcycle. Took off his helmet and started yelling at me." Then he focused on my face and said are you in a problem, should I drop you somewhere. I was so scared that without listening to what he said I ran away after walking about 2-3 kilometers I saw a Dhaba and moved there to use PCO for calling my mother as I called her someone picked up the call I said maa..maa... But nobody replied and then one voice came," whosoever is that side Nirmala Ji was found all burnt today early in the morning sorry to say she Is dead now I am sub-inspector Kartik, right now we are investigating because it seemed a murder case" hearing this I started crying on the call itself. Again a voice came can I know who are you?. With a sore throat, I replied I am Amrapali her daughter. The police officer asked me to reach there as soon as possible. I was so scared but he seemed to me that he could help me with my justice, I told him everything whatever happened to me since last night. After listening to this he said," don't go anywhere, stay wherever you are. I am coming to pick you up" I wasn't in that state that I could trust in him but still I believe in God and waited for him. After an hour he reached there and by with both hands on my shoulders, he took me in his jeep. Offered me water and said don't worry. I'll stand with you till the last and you'll surely get the Justice. Still, I was crying the whole way long after some time we reached to my house saw my mother's body lying in the room whole room was burnt. My mother was so burnt that she couldn't be identified. I tried to move more closer to her but the female constables didn't let me move in. I was screaming inadequately convincing myself. Then Mr. Kartik came to me and asked "whether I doubt anyone who could do this to my mother," I replied yes, my uncle and aunt are the evil ones since my father's death they always forced me and my mother to do things we never wanted. They did my marriage against my confirmation and always tried to suppress my mother's statements. Then I started telling the whole story from the day I got married till now. He said, "don't worry will find them out". They took my mother's body for postmortem. It was going to be night shortly. Mr. Kartik told me not to worry and move inside the house as for my security one Constable will be standing the whole night outside my house. From the very next he took me to the hospital for my tests and consult from the doctor and then we both started to find out all the people in this. Though it was a hard journey Mr. Kartik was someone who again made me believe that a good person still exists.

After 3 months of hard work shreds of evidence and witnesses, we concluded our fight for justice with a positive response from the court, and both the families were caught and prisoned outside the courtroom we congratulated us and I said him that " though I never studied too much and left my studies in between then to without having a bit knowledge of these things you were the only one who made me understand everything. Thank you so much, Mr. Kartik without you I would have never been a so strong woman. He answered," no Amrapali Ji you are strong enough just you needed a person on whom you can trust. Which you never got in your life, but now I am here you can call me whenever you want". After listening to this I couldn't control my feelings and hugged him tightly a few seconds after he too did. Then we realized that we are outside the courtroom,immediately we got apart from each other with an awkward smile. We both chose our way. And suddenly he came running towards my Autoricksaw and said Amrapali will you spent rest of your life with me and marry me......!

(To be continued.....)

Note From The Author :-

This book is just a piece of truth which is nowdays carrried out in different families. The story is just to tell you all, that rain doesn't falls whole year there is bright sunshine hiding under those dark clouds. Even if things are going worse you have the power to shine like rainbow after the rainfall.

www.ingramcontent.com/pod-product-compliance
Lightning Source LLC
Chambersburg PA
CBHW070206160726
47997CB00017B/1540